The

Chapter 1: Magic .... page 2

Chapter 2: Footprints.............. .... page 9

Chapter 3: What's That Sound? .... page 16

Chapter 4: The Cats of Comet Street .... page 21

Chapter 5: Found .... page 25

Written by Adam and Charlotte Guillain

RISING ★ STARS

Chapter 1: Magic

Tess, Rav, Asha and Finn were playing outside the flats when they noticed Stefan searching for something. "What are you looking for?" called Asha.

"Magic," replied Stefan, as he peered under the hedge.

"Magic?" repeated Finn. "That's strange!"

"It's the name of his cat!" giggled Tess.

"We'll help you!" said Rav. The friends began to search the play area.

"Why are you looking for him?" asked Asha.

"I haven't seen him since the day before yesterday," Stefan explained, and his face creased into a frown. "I think he's gone missing."

"Oh no!" cried Tess.

"He can't be far away," said Rav, scanning the car park.

"Yes, I bet someone round here's seen him," agreed Finn.

Stefan's face brightened a little. "Do you think so?"

"Let's make posters," suggested Asha. "We can put them up everywhere and then people will contact you if they've seen him."

Tess and Finn ran inside and returned with paper and pencils, and soon the friends were lying on the grass, drawing pictures of Magic on their posters. "Put my mum's phone number at the bottom for people to call – I know it off by heart," said Stefan.

Soon the posters were ready to be put up. "Magic looks different on every poster," Rav noticed.

"He's got the same blue collar though," said Stefan.

They stuck the posters up all around the flats and Rav walked down to the community centre with his mum to put one on the noticeboard.

"Now we have to wait," said Tess, sitting on one of the swings.

"What's that sound?" asked Finn and everyone froze. Finn was certain he could hear a very faint meow.

"I can't hear it – where's it coming from?" asked Rav, looking all around.

"There's Magic!" yelled Tess, jumping up.

A cat streaked past them and ran inside the flats. "Where did he go?" shouted Stefan as he rushed inside and sped up the stairs. They searched every floor and were about to give up when Asha heard a purring sound.

"Over here!" she called and the others rushed to join her.

Chapter 2: Footprints

A black cat was washing her paws beside a pot plant. "That's not Magic," sighed Stefan. "Magic has white paws."

Asha felt her excitement fizzle away to nothing.

"We'll find him," said Tess as they trudged back downstairs.

Outside, their neighbour, Mrs Robinson, was reading one of the posters.

"I haven't seen a cat," she told them, "but I did just see a rabbit hopping around."

"Skip – I must have left our gate open!" gasped Tess.

She dashed away, quickly followed by the others.

"There he is!" shouted Finn, pointing to the left.

Tess hurried across to where Skip was nibbling some grass. "That was close," she said, snatching him up.

"There's that meowing sound again," said Finn.

"I can't hear anything," said Rav. "Maybe you're imagining it?"

Tess returned Skip to her garden and shut the gate carefully.

"I have a feeling Magic isn't far away," said Asha reassuringly, but Stefan hung his head.

"What if he went off down the main road?" Stefan asked, a lump growing in his throat.

"I think cats normally stay close to home," said Tess. "Try not to worry."

Rav was staring at a wet, muddy patch on the ground. "Look at these footprints!" he called to the others. "Do you think they might be Magic's?" The others sprinted over and examined the footprints.

"There are more over here!" shouted Finn, beckoning the others over to the path.

"Maybe Magic ran past here when we were inside searching the flats?" suggested Asha, hurrying over to look and seeing that the trail of footprints led away from the play area to the other side of the flats.

"Magic!" called Stefan hopefully.

"The footprints stop here," sighed Rav, staring at the path.

"Wait, I can hear a voice," whispered Tess, and she tiptoed along the path.

"Good boy, now let's get those muddy paws cleaned up!" said the voice.

"Do you think someone's found Magic?" wondered Stefan, his face lighting up.

"Let's go and see!" said Finn, running around the corner.

Chapter 3: What's That Sound?

Finn sprinted around the bike shelter, the others close behind him. They all came to a halt at the sight of their neighbour, Jim. "Hi, you lot!" Jim said as he washed mud off his dog's paws. "Otto here just scampered through a muddy puddle so I'm cleaning him up before we go inside."

"Have you seen a black and white cat anywhere?" asked Asha.

"No, sorry," said Jim. "I've seen your posters and I'll keep a look out for him."

"Thanks," said Stefan, crouching down to stroke Otto.

As they headed back to the play area, they heard Stefan's mum shout his name.

Stefan!

"Maybe someone's contacted her about Magic?" said Asha.

Stefan raced to the gate but his face fell when his mum added, Lunchtime, come inside now, Stefan!"

"We'd better go in too, but let's meet after lunch and keep searching for Magic," said Finn.

"Okay," sighed Stefan. "Thanks for helping me."

After lunch, the friends gathered outside once more. "Where's your cap?" Finn asked Stefan. "I really like all the badges!"

"I took it off because it was making me feel too hot," Stefan told him.

"I'm sure I heard that strange mewing sound when I was in the garden eating lunch," said Finn.

"I couldn't hear it," said Tess, frowning.

"It was really faint!" said Finn. "Don't you believe me?"

"I've got an idea," said Rav quickly, before the twins started arguing. "Why don't we scatter some of Magic's cat treats around the flats?"

"We could try it," said Stefan, dashing inside to fetch the treats.

Chapter 4: The Cats of Comet Street

They began putting little piles of treats around the play area and the entrance to the flats. "Let's split up and keep watch for Magic," said Asha. Everyone ran off, leaving Finn beside the car park.

"There's that sound again!" he thought as he walked past the cars towards the garages.

A shape shot behind him and Finn spun around. A cat was busy munching the cat treats! "Stefan, is this Magic?" he shouted.

Stefan came racing around the corner but he skidded to a stop when he saw the cat. "No," he sighed. "We've found every single cat in Comet Street apart from Magic!"

Stefan led Finn around to the play area, where cats of all shapes and sizes were gobbling down cat treats. "I give up," said Stefan, slumping to the ground. Finn strode back to the car park to listen for the sound he'd heard and saw Mr and Mrs Edmunds were just driving in.

"Hello!" said Finn as Mr Edmunds climbed out of the car.

"Well, hello, Finn!" said his neighbour, smiling. "We've just returned from a couple of days away, visiting our grandchildren." Mrs Edmunds unloaded the luggage while Mr Edmunds unlocked the garage.

MEOW!

"There's that noise again!" yelled Finn.

Chapter 5: Found

Mr Edmunds stopped turning the key and listened with Finn.

MEOW!

"Stefan, come and listen to this!" shouted Finn. "Stefan's lost his cat," Finn explained to Mr Edmunds. "I think he must be really close by!"

Mr Edmunds heaved the garage door open …

… and a black animal leaped into Finn's arms. "Magic!" he gasped. Finn spun around and saw a grinning Stefan running towards him.

"You found him!" cried Stefan, gently taking Magic from Finn and nuzzling his pet.

"Oh dear, he must have got locked in the garage!" said Mr Edmunds.

"It doesn't matter," Stefan said, beaming. "We've found him now." The others sprinted over and crowded around to stroke Magic, then Stefan looked at Finn and said, "Wait here a minute!"

Stefan hurried inside with Magic, leaving everyone standing in the car park with Mr Edmunds.

"You must have very good hearing," Asha said to Finn. "None of us could hear Magic!"

"Sorry we didn't listen to you, Finn," Tess apologised.

Stefan burst out of the doors to the flats and hurried across to Finn.

"Thank you," he said, handing something to Finn.

"Wow, thanks!" said Finn. "I can use this for my school project."

Meanwhile, Mr Edmunds was counting the friends. "Just checking I don't shut one of you in the garage!" he said with a wink.

The Missing Cat

What other things will the Comet Street Kids collect
for their holiday challenge? Read the other books
in this band to find out!

The Missing Cat

Moonquake

Brilliant Braille

Stop Shouting!

Stranded Panda

A Midsummer Night's Disaster

Talk about the story

Answer the questions:

1 Why did Stefan say he was looking for his cat?

2 What does the word 'scanning' mean? (page 4) Can you think of another word that could be used instead?

3 Why was Rav 'staring at a wet, muddy patch on the ground' on page 13?

4 What was the name of Jim's dog?

5 Why did the friends start putting treats around the flats?

6 At the end of the story, Mr and Mrs Edmunds drove in. Where had they been?

7 Can you describe in your own words what the friends did to find Magic?

8 Do you have a family pet? Did you give it a name or did it already have one? If you had a cat, what would you name it?

Can you retell the story in your own words?